When

Beauty

Blooms

A NOVELETTE

By Victoria Lynn

When Beauty Blooms

Copyright ©2018 by Victoria Lynn

Cover Design by Victoria Lynn Designs www.victorialynndesigns.com
All rights reserved

Scroll vector for cover and interior: <a
href='https://www.freepik.com/free-vector/vintage-wedding-
frame_1108773.htm'>Designed by Freepik</a>

Copy-edit by Bridget Marshal

Published by Ichthus Family Productions

Printed in the USA

Website: www.victorialynnauthor.com

To those who don't know that they are beautiful, just the way God created them to be.

1774, Uxbridge, England

Being short was such a burden.

Marjorie Kirk leaned over the rail of the portico that graced the manor where she and her companions dwelt on the outskirts of London, and strained to see what her two companions were viewing.

"He's incredibly handsome," Daphne simpered, and her freckles bounced beneath her dimples as she smiled.

Marjorie noticed that her other friend, Ginger, looked wistfully over the edge of the balustrade and her eyes seemed to be searching for someone in particular. Miss Claire, their chaperone, only looked on with a soft smile of benevolence.

Her heart fluttered as she stood on tiptoe to see over the edge. Being short was a cross she must bear alone, as her other friends were gracefully tall and willowy. Her corset pinched painfully when she craned her neck to see who on earth the girls were talking about. "Where?" she gasped, trying to be graceful in her quest to see, but feeling incredibly awkward instead.

"There, the man with the chestnut-brown hair that waves off his forehead in a most attractive manner." Daphne fluttered her hand in front of her face in lieu of a fan as a blush suffused her pale, freckled skin with red. Daphne was a doll, but she was also a goose. She loved to flirt and often found herself talking people to death.

All Marjorie could see was the top of a few heads from her vantage point until they disappeared out of sight below the portico the girls stood upon. She fell back on her heels and drew a breath with a hand to her side in a hope to relieve her pinched ribs. Disappointment was overwhelming. Being the homeliest of the young ladies made her the one who was always lagging behind the others. She was the group's wallflower and often spent most of her time during parties with their chaperone, Miss Claire, since no one seemed to want to dance with a girl like Marjorie when the outgoing and vivacious Daphne or the mysterious and beautifully languid Ginger were around.

It wasn't by choice. She wished that others would take notice of her. Even the visiting ladies seemed to snub their noses at her, or more commonly, ignore her completely. She was too much of a lady to stick her nose where it wasn't wanted, and she was too shy to strike up a conversation with a stranger. She had been that way her whole life, and no amount of boarding school training had taken that out of her. That is where she had met her three companions. They had gone to finishing school together, and they formed such a bond, that the parents and guardians had been coerced into agreeing to let them stay together, collectively hiring Miss Claire to chaperone them all in their quest for mates and lives of their own. If there was one thing that all of the girls had in common, it was family or guardians who would rather let someone else take the responsibility for their welfare.

Miss Claire cast a benevolent look over her charges, her eyes sweeping them and their attire for a hair or bow out of place. She nodded with satisfaction until her eyes snagged on Marjorie's. They held each other's gaze, and Miss Claire offered a comforting smile. Marjorie found great comfort in her close friendship with her chaperone. Most ladies would scoff at such a relationship with a woman of greater age who had never married and seemed to have no prospects, and was a chaperone no less. But Marjorie cherished the friendship, and the wisdom she gleaned from Miss Claire was unparalleled. The woman had a quiet way of comforting Marjorie's troubled heart and encouraging her with just a look or a smile.

Another carriage pulled slowly up the rounded gravel drive and drew to a stop before the grand entrance below. Marjorie bumped her shoulder with Ginger's elbow as they both leaned over to catch a look. Ginger gasped and fluttered a hand to her chest, and Marjorie looked up to see a blush suffuse the girl's cheeks.

"Are you all right, Ginger?" she asked kindly, patting her friend on the back.

Ginger turned brown eyes that were full of light on her friend and Marjorie's heart jumped with joy at the joy on Ginger's face. "It's Papa. He came." Her words were a near whisper, and without another glance she turned and disappeared inside.

Marjorie was so happy for her friend. Ginger had been longing to see her father, who had been traveling abroad for years on matters of state. She had been expectantly waiting for him to come in answer to the invitation she had sent, but had been doubtful, as he was a very busy man.

"Well, no use staying up here any longer. I may as well get to meet the handsome young men as they come in instead of just watching them arrive." Daphne tossed her head and the one red curl that fell over her shoulder bounced. Apparently, she was already bored with their game of watching. She never stayed focused on anything very long. Her aunt and uncle were the owners of this estate and the ones who threw the lavish parties in an effort to find a husband for their niece and her two friends. Aside from wanting the best for Daphne, they had spoiled her with a lavish lifestyle, which was more than could be said for Marjorie. Marjorie only wished that she had a family that loved her the way Daphne's did. Even if they were away on holiday most of the time, leaving the girl to the chaperone they had hired.

Daphne swept from the portico while straightening her pink dress. It was a fashion faux pas for a girl with red hair to wear pink. However, Daphne never was one to follow convention. In her mind, rules were meant to be broken, and she often vociferated this freely. Which gave Miss Claire quite the conundrum when it came to being the high-strung young woman's chaperone.

Miss Claire rolled her eyes at Daphne for Marjorie's benefit before giving her a wink and sweeping after the redhead, leaving Marjorie alone on the portico. Now that she was alone, she looked both ways before walking to the side of the portico that overlooked the side of the house where the garden and grounds were located. Gathering her skirts up, she sat on the brick floor and dangled her legs around a spindle, letting her feet hang and swing, much like she had done often as a little girl. The garden was a beautiful view this time of year. Perhaps she wouldn't attend the party after all. What was the use? The other girls twitted her, none of the men paid her any attention, and all she would do was sit watching the others' gaiety like an old maid. Not that she resented old maids. Miss Claire was a dear, but the wish of Marjorie's heart was to be a wife and mother. But to be one of those, she would have to be noticed. She swung her legs back and forth, delighting in the freedom to break convention, if only for a moment. Looking out over the garden was one of her keenest delights and she had a lovely view from where she sat.

"Excuse me, miss?" A masculine voice from below frightened her out of her reverie. She stuck her head between two of the spindles and looked down. A man stood below her, looking up with a confused and slightly amused look on his face. He was a young man and he held his hat in his hand and the handle of his cane was looped over his wrist.

Startled and mortified beyond belief, she pulled her legs up, her face hot with the realization her ankles and a scandalous amount of stockinged leg had been showing. Tears of embarrassment burned in her eyes and threatened to spill down her lightly powdered face. She had wanted to be noticed, but not like this. How embarrassing.

After pulling her legs back through the spindles, Marjorie attempted to stand, but tripped over her own skirts and tumbled to the floor with nothing but a mussed dress and a twisted ankle to show for her carelessness and hurry.

"Miss, are you all right? Might I be of assistance?" came the voice from below, but frightfully closer.

5

"I don't see at all how you could be of any help." Her tone was bitter and sharp as she fought to stand, despite the harsh pain in her ankle. Why must her skirts be all twisted around her shoes? And why couldn't she untangle them? Something sharp in her ankle gave way and she collapsed with a cry of pain.

It throbbed terribly, but through the haze of tears, she saw the man from below had scaled the trellis, clambered over the rail, and now knelt at her side. *What on earth?*

"Are you all right?" he asked, remaining at a respectful distance, but wringing his hands, as if he wanted to do something, but didn't dare.

If she was the least bit embarrassed before, it had just been multiplied by ten. Not only had he seen her in a most undignified state, but he had also seen her cry. Her worst nightmare had come true, and she couldn't even run away.

"Please, what do you want? Leave me alone . . ." Her voice broke and she struggled to right her skirts while on the ground and without twisting her ankle, which was nearly impossible.

He remained calm and just looked at her. "May I help you up?" He held out his hand.

She thought about it for a short moment then placed her hand in his. He lifted her by the elbows, and she winced, her left foot still caught in the skirt of her dress and bent at an awkward angle.

"Can you walk?" His voice was deep, and altogether oratorically lovely sounding.

She shook her head. How on earth to tell him that her foot was caught in the fabric of her dress?

He stood, awkwardly holding her upright, obviously unsure of what to do.

The urge to be completely unconventional once again rose in Marjorie. She was already mortified. She should just tell him and get this nasty business over with so she never had to see him again. The restraint snapped and she huffed. "My shoe is stuck on the fabric of my skirt, my ankle is twisted and I can't get it unstuck." A sob caught in the back of her throat. Just wonderful, why not blubber all over him as well?

"Can you dislodge it? Or shall I?" he asked kindly.

"I need to sit down." She gasped as he suddenly swept her up into his arms and deposited her on one of the chairs that sat on the portico with more care than grace. She scooped her skirt and numerous fluffy petticoats up in her arms and unhooked the heel of her shoe that had caught in a ruffle of one of the petticoats. She sighed with relief when she could straighten her leg again, but the pain in her ankle was alarming.

"You've gone pale; are you quite all right?" His voice sounded worried and since he had vaulted to her rescue, she could not convince herself to look into his face, being far too overwhelmed and thoroughly too embarrassed to do so.

With a nod, Marjorie stood to her feet, teetering a bit on her one good foot. She needed to limp to her room. The gentleman took her arm. Oh dear. The sound of conversation from downstairs that filtered through the open French doors was momentarily hushed and music began to play.

Remaining calm and collecting her emotions, Marjorie drew herself up straight. "The dancing has started, you must go down and join the party." She turned to look into his face. "I am sure you will be missed if –" her words trailed off. He was a young and fit specimen of a gentleman. Although, she shouldn't have expected anything different considering he had climbed the trellis and swung over the rail with ease. His square jaw was rather attractive, though he didn't have the blue eyes that the other girls swooned over. She shook her head. Enough of such thoughts.

"Marjorie! Here you are, I have been looking everywhere for –" Miss Claire came bustling out onto the portico, her brown colored dress billowing behind her and the silk making a heavy rustling sound. "Oh! Are you all right, dear?" She came rushing to Marjorie's side, casting a slightly suspicious glance in the young man's direction.

"I am fine, Miss Claire. I tripped and this man helped me." She quickly leaned her weight on the arm of her chaperone and deftly pulled her arm from his grasp.

"Well, we are indebted to you, I am sure." Miss Claire still had that protective look on her face. That of a mother bear protecting her cub. Marjorie could tell that she was analyzing the man with her eyes.

He bowed slightly.

Miss Claire must have approved because she turned her gaze to Marjorie with a questioning tilt to her eyebrows. "Are you sure you didn't hurt yourself?"

"Well, I did twist my ankle a bit . . . ," Marjorie begrudgingly admitted. Though she may have understated it a mite. She was still clenching her jaw in an effort not to cry when she moved suddenly. But she did give Miss Claire a look that begged her not to draw any more undue attention to her. They had been friends for so long that often just a look sufficed to share their thoughts and wishes with each other.

Miss Claire nodded. "I see. Let me escort you to your room and we can freshen you up a bit. I hope you don't mind, sir, that I leave you to see yourself down to the party?"

He bowed again. "Of course not. I hope the lady is well." He bobbed his head in a subtle bow to Marjorie, picked up his hat and cane from where he had dropped them on the portico floor and quickly strode from the scene.

The iron in Marjorie's spine melted and she wilted against Miss Claire.

"Come dear, let's get you to your room. Doctor Bennet is a guest downstairs, thank heaven, and I will discreetly fetch him to tend to your ankle."

With much pain and a good bit of awkward maneuvering, they finally got Marjorie to her bedchamber where she fell back on the bed, flushed and exhausted.

"I've never been more embarrassed in my life!" she wailed, burying her face in the pillows while Miss Claire lifted her feet to the bed.

"Now dear, I am sure it wasn't all that bad," her friend consoled quietly.

"You have no idea!" It was all Marjorie could do not to burst into tears. "I made a complete and utter fool of myself.

I sat on the portico and swung my legs over the edge while straddling a rail."

The silence that met this statement caused Marjorie to poke her head from beneath the silk ruffles of the pillow and glance at her friend. Miss Claire had a surprised look on her face for a moment, then it quickly dissolved into one of containment with pressed lips. She turned quickly but Marjorie caught the twinkle in her eye. "I see" was all she said.

"I thought no one was around and my ankles were shamefully in view, I admit."

"Mmhmm."

"Don't you understand? He saw me! He was standing below in the garden. I thought I would die of mortification when he called out to me and I realized he was standing below." Marjorie laid a hand over her eyes. It was all too much. Recounting it was almost as painful as living it in the first place.

"I am sure he didn't see much, dear. One can't, you know, looking up at the portico from that distance." Miss Claire glided to the corner where she pulled the bell rope that connected to the servants' quarters.

Marjorie wasn't believing it for one minute. "He had to have! And then, when I pulled my legs back and tried to stand, my heel was caught on one of these confounded petticoats and I tripped all over myself."

Miss Claire turned sharply and returned to the bed, a questioning look on her face. "If you were on the portico and he was below, how did he get to be helping you up?"

"He climbed the trellis and clambered over the railing."

Miss Claire ducked and carefully divested Marjorie's foot of its shoe.

"Ouch!" She bit her lip against the pain.

"Oh! I'm sorry." Miss Claire held the shoe in her hand, her lips quivering.

Marjorie felt betrayed. "You are trying not to smile!" Her tone was incredulous.

Miss Claire shook her head vigorously. "Of course I wouldn't do –"

"Don't try to deny it! I saw you!" Marjorie was quite incensed.

And with that, Miss Claire burst into a bout of uncontrollable laughter.

Marjorie pouted. "The very idea," she fumed.

"I – I am so sorry, Marjorie . . . just the idea, and the way you were so disgusted with yourself, you should have seen your face!" Miss Claire pulled herself together, took a deep breath, and shook out Marjorie's stocking.

Marjorie held her tongue in an offended silence. A knock at the door brought her to a sitting position and she straightened her dress as best as possible in the moment. Miss Claire answered the door, spoke quietly for a few moments, then returned to the bedside.

"I sent Anna for Doctor Bennet. She said she saw him below and that he was in the parlor."

11

Marjorie ignored her, the throbbing in her ankle making her just want to cry.

"Marjorie?" Miss Claire spoke softly. "I hope you aren't angry with me. You know I didn't mean anything bad by my amusement. It was just so, well, amusing." She chuckled again, but stopped when Marjorie continued to ignore her.

Marjorie already felt stupid enough, like an utter fool, and to have her very real feelings laughed at by Miss Claire, it was too much to bear. The only thing she wanted in the moment was sympathy, and that was the farthest thing from what she was receiving. It might be silly of her, but she wasn't trying to be petty. It just smarted a bit.

Miss Claire drew a breath and schooled her features. "I'm sorry, Marjorie . . ." A soft note of disappointment and reproof entered her tone and she picked up a shawl from the foot of the bed and wound it around Marjorie's shoulders. "Dear, I think you might be overreacting just a little. It was nothing that won't be forgotten shortly in the future. And from the looks of the young man, I can tell you he probably thinks you did nothing wrong and that he rescued a damsel in distress. And I think that you will find it somewhat amusing yourself sometime in the near future. Perhaps tomorrow."

Miss Claire's calm voice and her gently reproving words pulled Marjorie from her pouting. "I'm sorry, Miss Claire, I just . . . I was so embarrassed and . . . Well, it still feels more substantial of a humiliation than you say, but I suppose you are right. You usually are."

Miss Claire returned the smile that Marjorie offered her and she was pleased to see that she had patched up the small rift in their friendship.

Doctor Bennet was kind, attentive, and told her that she had sprained her ankle. Sprained quite badly he was afraid. She would be laid up for a few days at least, after which she could hobble about with the help of a cane.

Marjorie missed the party that night. She finally convinced Miss Claire to go downstairs and enjoy herself, if only to keep an eye on Daphne, who no doubt needed some help in the department of propriety.

The girls were so sympathetic when they popped in after the party to have a late evening chat in their nightgowns. They clambered into Marjorie's bed, careful not to jar the injured ankle. Daphne spoke much about the various virtues of the men she had met, and Ginger could barely get a word in edgewise, but when she did, it was of her father. Marjorie was happy for both of her friends. Happy that they had enjoyed their evening, but part of her had that same, old feeling of being left behind and useless. No one had a need for her; she hadn't even been missed at the party. When the girls had gone and Miss Claire had bid her goodnight, Marjorie heaved a sigh and settled deeper into her silk pillows. Loneliness engulfed her feelings. Marjorie had not had the most enjoyable of childhoods. Growing up an orphan and being raised by an aunt and uncle who didn't see you as much more than a burden until they could one day marry you off had been trying to say the least. Daphne had been raised a spoiled child, loved and petted by all. Ginger, though distant from her parents at times due to business and the travel involved, still spoke of her parents in such glowing terms and you could see it in her eyes the love she bore for them and they for her.

Marjorie had no such feelings. Aunt Gertrude and Uncle George had sent her to numerous boarding and finishing schools until she had been too old for them. Then, while they traveled the continent, she was put in the care of Miss Claire in the hopes that she would discover a husband of some kind. Preferably one who could pay the dowry. Marjorie, of course, wasn't out for a fortune, but money enough to take her from beneath her uncle's reluctant care would be more than welcome.

She rolled over, attempting to simultaneously keep her nightgown and bed clothes from getting tangled. Miss Claire always encouraged her that God knew and He cared, but sometimes He felt so far away. Why couldn't her life just work out in a way that would be pleasant? Why did things have to be so hard?

Sunday morning, Marjorie allowed herself to be primped and curled for church. Somehow the hairstyles of the day made her round face look more round than it actually was. And of course, the corset and dress she wore was enough to drive anyone mad. "Shall I pull your laces now, miss?" Anna, the maid, asked demurely.

Marjorie sighed in resignation. "I suppose, since there is no way around it. We must either conform to fashion or be outcasts, and I am enough of the latter without making matters worse by not having my corset tight enough."

Anna looked confused by Marjorie's thoughts on fashion. "Miss?"

"Never mind, Anna, just tighten the laces, please."

Anna ducked her head in a nod and reached for the laces that were comfortably loose on Marjorie's corset. Marjorie grasped the bed post in an effort to brace herself. Anna pulled, making Marjorie wince and inwardly growl at the way fashion had degraded womankind. She bit her tongue to keep anything bitter from flying from her mouth . . . a worthy quality she often admired in Miss Claire.

When Anna had tortured Marjorie enough and constrained her ribs and waist to impossible quarters, she tied them off and helped Marjorie on with the rest of her clothes. Pannier, petticoats, skirt, stomacher, and doublet. Since it was a church affair, she also wrapped the kerchief around her neck. If anything made Marjorie look plump, the far too fluffy kerchief made her even more so.

"There you are, miss. Is that to your satisfaction?" Anna folded her hands in front of her and looked expectantly at her charge.

Marjorie gave herself the once-over in the mirror and tried not to glower. The color navy was pretty enough on her; indeed, it seemed to set off her amber eyes. But everything else conspired against her figure. Any good looks she had were overwhelmed by the volume and unflattering cut of the gown.

"That will do, Anna, thank you." Marjorie took the cane that had been her constant companion for the last few days, gathered her reticule onto her wrist and limped out of the room and down the hall.

Ginger met her at the top of the stairs. "Let me help you, Marjorie."

Marjorie took her friend's arm and allowed herself to be helped down the curving staircase. Trying to forget herself, she looked up at Ginger and noted the hopeful, yet melancholy, look in her lovely honey-brown eyes.

"What is it, Ginger?"

"I'm sorry?"

"Are you all right?" Marjorie pressed.

Ginger smiled and gave a soft little laugh that was gentle and made her a success with the gentlemen. "Of course, I am all right, why do you ask?"

"I can see it in your eyes. I know you better than you think, Ginger. We haven't been companions for these two years without getting to know one another."

A slightly pained expression crossed Ginger's face. "Of course."

"So what is it?"

"I haven't heard from Father yet. He said he would write and let me know if I could come up to London to be with him and Mother or not. It has been four days since the party, and I haven't heard yet." Worry creased Ginger's forehead.

Marjorie patted Ginger's arm. "You know how dreadfully slow the post can be, dear. I am sure it will arrive soon. I'll pray that God gives the courier wings!" Marjorie rubbed the spot on Ginger's arm that was beneath the lace ruffle at the end of her elbow-length sleeves. "I know you miss them, darling."

Ginger ducked her head, but not before Marjorie saw a few tears gathering in the corner of her eyes. Marjorie was about to mentally reprimand herself for making her friend cry when

Ginger looked up with a grateful and more relieved look. "Thank you, Marjorie. Really. That means more than you probably realize."

Marjorie opened her mouth to reply, light shining in her heart at the words of her friend.

"Does this dress make me look fat?" Daphne glided down the stairs, her purple gown flowing behind her. Marjorie glared. Not only did Daphne look like a stick in her dress, she also had just ruined a sweet moment between her and her friend.

"Did you even look in the mirror, Daphne?" Marjorie tried to keep the bite from her tone, but failed.

Daphne looked at her as if Marjorie had suddenly sprouted another head. "But of course! What girl doesn't look in the mirror before leaving the house?"

Marjorie rolled her eyes, but she wasn't going to let the girl make her mad. Daphne could try the soul of a saint. She pressed her lips together.

"Well? Does it make me look fat?" Daphne spun in a slow circle for them.

Ginger gave Marjorie a look of sympathy and rolled her eyes. "Of course not, Daphne, though, the purple might be a bit bright for church . . ."

"Nonsense! What is church for, if not to be noticed?" Daphne tossed her red curls.

"Perhaps to worship God?"

"Oh, that, of course I will be worshiping God! Can't one do that in purple as well as in grey, brown, or navy blue?"

Ginger just shook her head. "I am sure it has nothing to do with the new minister we have the pleasure of meeting today." The sarcasm that dripped from her soft voice was not without kindness. Marjorie didn't know how she did it sometimes.

There was no doubt about it, that color on Daphne was quite stunning. Marjorie just wasn't sure if it was in an attractive way or a noticeable way.

Miss Claire joined the group and looked askance at Daphne. "Purple?" was all she said as she raised an eyebrow.

"It's what I felt like wearing today," Daphne replied innocently with another toss of her head as she stretched out her neck, admiring herself in the hall mirror.

"I see." Miss Claire smoothed her demure, soft-grey silk and checked her timepiece. "We must scurry, ladies, if we are going to be in time for services. I have heard that the new reverend, William Baeley, is quite punctual and it will not do to be late on our first meeting."

The carriage ride was full of Daphne primping and Ginger and Marjorie trying not to laugh at her antics and spontaneous comments. When they arrived at the church, the footman helped each of the ladies from the vehicle and he escorted Marjorie up the steps and to her seat because of her ankle. It still hurt, though not nearly as severely as it had the first few days.

She took her seat and let the girls squeeze into the pew next to her. She placed her bad foot up on the kneeler. Hopefully, elevating it would alleviate some of the swelling for the time being. She was arranging the folds of her dress when the minister stepped out of the vestry and towards the pulpit. She craned her neck, eager along with the others to see the new minister for the first time.

To her shock and horror, low and behold, it was the man who had climbed the trellis and rescued her on the veranda. She could feel a blush working its way up her cheeks, but when he took his pulpit and looked directly at her, she felt herself heat to the point where she knew she must be scarlet. Their eyes locked, and she wished she could disappear. How utterly embarrassing. She couldn't have said what the message of the sermon was for she was far too flustered. And Daphne leaning over in the midst of the dissertation to whisper, "Isn't he positively adorable?" in her ear didn't help in the least bit. Red-faced and absolutely flustered, it was all she could do to bite her tongue.

When they arrived home from church, they were stopped in the entryway by the butler with a letter for Ginger.

Marjorie watched her friend flush with pleasure and take the missive from the silver platter. "Thank you, Watkins." She looked about her for a moment as if asking permission to open the letter.

"Open it, Ginger! I am dying with curiosity!" Daphne dramatically raised a hand to her forehead in excitement.

Ginger barely smiled.

"Do open it, Ginger, dear," Marjorie consoled her.

Ginger carefully slit open the envelope with a hairpin she had pulled from her neatly coiffed hair. Her hands were trembling slightly as she withdrew the missive. When she had unfolded the sheet of paper, her face lit up with joy. "It is from Papa!" She read it quickly, and her face grew even brighter and more joyful, if that was even possible. With a sigh and a tear that slowly worked its way from the corner of her eye, she placed the letter over her heart and looked at the floor while blinking rapidly in an effort to stem the flow of tears.

"What is it?" Marjorie placed a hand on her friend's arm, concerned, but excited.

"Papa has asked me to come and live in London with him and Mama. At long last!" She smiled widely and wrapped her arms around Marjorie, swinging her in a circle, their skirts flying. Marjorie laughed and ducked her head in an effort to hide the fact that her ankle hurt. She didn't want to ruin Ginger's lovely moment, especially not with something so trivial.

Marjorie stilled the twirl and embraced Ginger with a kiss on the cheek. "You sweet dear! I am so happy for you!" As the words left her mouth, a bit of hurt pricked her own heart. Another person was leaving her. Moving on with their life and leaving her behind. She wished with all her heart that she had parents who wanted her to spend time with them.

The girls helped ready Ginger for her trip. It would be a few days before she departed, but they had much to pack. Especially since Daphne, flighty soul that she was, had a talent for giving gifts.

"You must take this one! It will look smashing on you! It will be all the rage in London." Daphne held a blush-pink ball gown against herself and twirled in front of the mirror, admiring the gown and showing it off to her two friends.

"I couldn't possibly take three of your dresses, Daphne, don't be silly. You've already given me two." Ginger shook her head as she laid a pile of handkerchiefs carefully in the tray of the large trunk that was spread open before her.

"I am not being silly! I can just as easily get another, and this blush color is just the thing to set off your brunette beauty! I insist. You shall have more ample chance to enjoy it than I would. Balls are few and far between here, while in London I hear most of society indulges in one nearly every night. And with your father being a diplomat, I can see him taking you to many a function, and it would not do at all to wear a gown more than once. It could spell disaster if a suitor thought you were poor!"

Marjorie tried to hide a giggle. For all of Daphne's ridiculous ideas, she was a loveable little goose.

Ginger looked slightly resigned . . . "Oh, all right, if you insist."

"I do." Daphne did her best to fold the dress, but it ended up looking more like a wad than a folded garment as she dumped it into the trunk. Marjorie scooped it up and rescued it, smoothing out the wrinkles and folding it neatly.

"Oh! And of course, you must take the headpiece that matches . . . You will be the belle of the ball! I'll go and fetch it." Daphne dashed from the room in a more excited than ladylike manner.

Ginger sighed and sat down on the bed, a few garments clutched in her hands. She smiled and shook her head. "What am I going to do with her?"

Marjorie returned the smile and sat down on the bed next to her friend. "Just love her, as always." She placed her arm around Ginger's waist and rested her chin against her shoulder. "I am going to miss you."

"And I you." Ginger returned the embrace. "Thank you for being such a good friend, Marjorie. I shall miss your company. Your . . . friendship."

Marjorie fought at the tears that came to her eyes. She was the farthest thing from a good friend, but it felt good to hear it from someone she had come to love. "You will write, won't you?"

"Of course! To you, Daphne, and Miss Claire. I shall miss you all. Perhaps I can even convince Father to have all of you up for a long visit to London, it's not that far after all. Wouldn't you like that, dear?"

The idea of visiting a place so full of people, where parties and social functions were as frequent as breathing quite honestly frightened her more than she cared to admit. "Oh, well, of course, I am sure we would enjoy it." Her words were somewhat hesitant as her mind was thinking exactly the opposite.

"Oh, you would, darling." Ginger jumped up and folded the rest of the items that she held in her lap and placed them in the trunk. "I am so excited!" She gave a sedate little jump that set her skirts to swishing.

Marjorie chuckled. Ginger almost never broke her serenity; she must be very excited.

"I'm back! Here it is!" Daphne waved the headpiece above her head, sending the feather that was a part of the adornment to fluttering. It had a blush rose and a string of pearls that would indeed match the gown to perfection.

"Thank you so much, Daphne. I was just telling Marjorie that perhaps I could convince Father to have you girls up to London for a holiday."

"Wonder upon wonders! That would be simply marvelous! I already can't wait! I must get a new dress, or a few. But, Ginger, dear, what is Marjorie going to do? She hates society." Daphne prattled on, suddenly even more excited than usual.

"What?" Ginger asked, glancing back and forth between Daphne and the now bright-red Marjorie.

"Well, you know. She is always silent as a mouse and can't seem to mix with people, no matter how hard she tries."

Daphne's blunt words, though true, still rankled in Marjorie's heart. She could feel the blush that heated her cheeks. How embarrassing. Must her life constantly be surrounded by humiliation and embarrassment?

"Daphne!" Ginger scolded while looking between Marjorie and Daphne in a concerned manner.

"What? It's true, isn't it? She hates parties."

Marjorie felt the blush on her cheeks deepen.

"Why don't we let Marjorie speak for herself." Miss Claire entered the room, a pile of laundered clothing hanging from her arm. Marjorie thanked the heavens for her entrance. Miss Claire could always bring wisdom to a situation and she was the ultimate peacekeeper, though often Daphne was the one who started fires that she needed to put out.

Daphne tossed her head and became transfixed on straightening the feather on the headpiece she held in her hands.

Ginger and Miss Claire both looked at her, waiting for her answer. Marjorie was at a loss of what to say. Should she admit that social events made her nervous? That she couldn't abide that many people for very long? That she was, in short, a failure at being a proper lady? Or should she lie?

One should never lie.

"Well, I don't exactly find as much pleasure in parties as you do, but . . ." She sighed. "They make me nervous."

"See! What did I tell you?" Daphne sounded triumphant.

"Daphne." Miss Claire's remonstrance was direct and efficient.

Daphne huffed.

Marjorie felt the tears start to her eyes. Daphne was being so insensitive. It had been hard for Marjorie to speak the truth in so direct a way. It was hard for her that her friends were so gifted in the social graces – far above even the average young lady – and she was so exempt from any wit, charm, or grace in the public setting.

Ginger made the ideal diplomat's daughter. Calm, serene, a splendid conversationalist, well-read, demure . . . the list could go on.

And Daphne was popular at social functions with her flattery, her energy, her excitement, and generosity. Not to mention her good looks. Half the young men sought her company at any party or excursion.

In Marjorie's eyes, she herself lacked all of the above virtues that her friends possessed. Admitting her inadequacies was an uncomfortable position to say the least.

"Now, girls, I expect you to give Marjorie some space. Each person has their own likes, dislikes, and personalities. We shouldn't taunt others about what we perceive as deficiencies in their characters. It would be wiser to look at our own and examine and correct those before we discourage another by our opinions." Miss Claire looked pointedly at Daphne, who was blushing, as she laid out the articles of clothing she had brought in. "I have a few items that need my immediate attention, I shall leave you girls to finish helping Ginger pack." She gave one more warning glance in Daphne's direction before she swept from the room.

Daphne turned upon Marjorie the instant the door closed behind Miss Claire. "Darling," she effused. "I am so terribly sorry, I didn't mean in the least to taunt you. Honest I didn't!" Real contrition was visible in Daphne's pale, freckled face as she held out her hands to Marjorie.

Marjorie's heart melted at once. One couldn't stay mad at Daphne long. Her faults, though hurtful at times, were not intentional and her manner so winning and contrite that she was easy to forgive, for though she made mistakes, she was a very repentant sinner. Marjorie sighed. After all, it wasn't as if Daphne's comments were full of venom in the least. It had been her own insecurities that had made her feel so degraded.

Sweeping her friend into a hug, she buried the feelings of insecurity that sought to plague her. Now was not the time to dwell on them. "I forgive you, Daphne, I know you didn't mean it that way. I am sorry if I was a bit upset. That was my own fault, not yours."

"Yes, but I was being quite stupid. And I should have known not to twit you about it." Daphne returned the hug with much vigor.

Marjorie exchanged a smiling and sympathetic look with Ginger. They started upon the handkerchief pile, folding them carefully when they were once again interrupted by Daphne.

She gasped and threw her hands in the air. "I have an idea! Oh, Marjorie, this will be wonderful!" She giggled and clapped her hands, turning in a circle, much like a little child.

"What is it now, Daphne?" Ginger asked with a quiet and patient voice.

"Oh! It is a fabulous idea!"

Ginger shared an eye roll with Marjorie. "Do tell."

"We can teach Marjorie how to behave at parties!"

Marjorie winced. As if she didn't know how to behave. Daphne's choice of words often left much to be desired. "I am sure she is quite capable of behaving like a lady, Daphne," Ginger scolded.

"Oh, you know what I meant. How to play the society girl!"

That's exactly what it would be, playing.

Ginger's eyes lit with interest. "We could give her a few ideas on how to make conversation."

"Exactly!" Daphne squeaked. "And dress her up for the occasion too! I have just the dress!"

Marjorie grew instantly timid. "Oh, I am sure I have something serviceable." What could the girl be thinking? Not much of Daphne's wardrobe would fit Marjorie in the least.

"Serviceable? Pah." Daphne frowned in disgust. "She must have something splendid."

Marjorie was now embarrassed. "Daphne, it won't fit."

Daphne cast a glance from Marjorie's head to her toes and Marjorie had to resist the urge to smooth her dress. But her friend waved her hand as if it were nothing. "You needn't worry, one of my fair accomplishments is that I am quite skilled with the needle, and the dress I am speaking of has plenty of room to be let out and altered."

"Before tomorrow night?" Marjorie was still doubtful.

Daphne tossed her curls. "My dear, you underestimate my talent. I am far superior to even the best seamstress in all of England." She put on a theatrical air and raised a hand dramatically to her forehead, causing her companions to giggle.

"What about France?" Ginger asked mischievously. Marjorie had to stifle a giggle. France was still the pinnacle of fashion.

"Tut tut, never mind that, I said England," Daphne hissed before resuming her pose. "Now," just as quickly, she melted into a seat on the bed, causing some of the handkerchiefs they had painstakingly folded to come undone. "Let's get down to business."

Marjorie wandered outside, her mind spinning with conversation starters, rules of etiquette, and ways to flirt with her fan. Ginger and Daphne had drilled her for hours. Tomorrow they would spend some more time talking of how to be socially adept while Daphne sewed the dress she was set on Marjorie wearing. A small amount of confidence was rising in Marjorie; she was starting to think that she might be able to do this after all.

She strolled through the garden, limping slightly on her sore ankle, but enjoying the feel of the breeze through her hair as it played about her skirts and fluttered the ribbons of her bonnet. She had missed this. The simple pleasure of a stroll had been denied her for more than a week due to the injury to her ankle and she couldn't begin to express how much pleasure she derived from it now. The hollyhocks and roses would be in full bloom in a week or so, and their tightly wound buds whispered of the promise of beauty that would burst forth soon. The promise of that beauty was almost as enjoyable as the beauty itself, Marjorie often thought. While her friends had been training themselves on how to act at a social function, she had been enjoying her studies and the beauty of nature.

She loved flowers and often liked to keep a garden when she could. Growing roses was one of her greatest pleasures. They were difficult, finicky, and downright difficult to grow, but under just the right circumstances they would bloom in a bounty of beauty that made even the hardest of hearts gasp in awe.

A cry of pain arrested her attention and progress down the cobblestoned pathway. It came again and her innate sense of mothering took over. She gathered her skirts into her hands and dashed off the path and towards the sound.

It was seven-year-old Marcus, the son of the housekeeper and butler, the married couple who ran the house and grounds and had for years. He was sitting on the turf and holding his leg while manfully attempting to keep from crying.

"Marcus! What is it? Are you all right?" Marjorie fell to her knees next to him, trying not to grimace at the pain in her ankle from running. She probably shouldn't have run on it yet.

He gulped. "My leg hurts."

Marjorie took in the scene around her, the tree above, the broken tree branch and the scraped hands of little Marcus. "Here, let me see."

She took a deep breath and placed her hands on his leg. She ran her hand along it, examining it for anything amiss. "I don't think anything is broken, little one. Here, shhhh . . . It's all right." She pulled him into a hug and cuddled his head while he let the tears tumble down his face.

She realized that her run had taken her quite a ways from the house, and while she might be able to carry Marcus a small distance, with her ankle and the length they were from the house . . . it might not be possible. Someone cleared their throat behind her and both she and Marcus jumped and whirled to see who had made the noise.

Not again.

It was the new minister. William Baeley. Any chance of remotely impressing him had certainly been dead and buried the moment he found her with dangling legs around the spindles in the portico railing. She sighed. The good Lord above must have decided that she needed some humbling. But this felt like too much.

"May I be of some assistance, Miss Kirk?"

She slowly stood, taking the time to school her features to be completely composed, which was exactly what she wasn't feeling right now. She brushed at the green patches near the knees on her skirt and turned.

Though her face must be bright red and her heart was positively beating out of her chest, she gave a demure little curtsey. "Thank you, Reverend Baeley. I would greatly appreciate some assistance. Little Marcus has fallen from the tree and –"

"I'm not little," came the little voice, half swallowed by tears from behind them.

Marjorie turned and softly smoothed back the hair from the boy's face. "Of course not, I'm sorry, Marcus. You must excuse me." She smiled at him. She felt comfortable around little ones, but having to associate with other adults is where she ran into problems. *Lord, help me keep my calm.*

She turned back to Mr. Baeley. "Would you be willing to carry him to the house? He seems to have injured his leg and scraped up his hands quite badly. I am afraid I wouldn't be able to take him to the house myself."

He nodded solemnly and knelt on one knee beside the boy. He bowed before the little boy. "Your majesty, may I offer my humble self to your service and carry you, as befits a king, to the house?"

He was so serious that Marjorie couldn't tell if he was joking or not.

The little boy nodded just as solemnly and Marjorie bent to help support the little bruised leg as Mr. Baeley lifted him carefully in his arms.

Marjorie tried to keep up and she carried on a bit of conversation with Marcus to distract him from the possible pain. He winced several times when Mr. Baeley accidentally jostled him. It was hard for her to talk with Mr. Baeley present, but he was so silent, that she soon slipped into her usual comfortable self when she was talking with children.

She gasped for breath ere long and limped a few steps as she had stepped on a stone that had jolted her ankle.

"Can you keep up, Miss Kirk?"

"Yes, indeed. I'm sorry."

She had been speaking to Marcus, but it was the only words they spoke to each other on what seemed like a long walk back to the house.

When they finally reached the house, Marjorie led them into the parlor where she pulled the settee forward for Mr. Baeley to lay Marcus on.

The little boy whimpered when the minister set him down.

"There, there, Marcus. Can you wait here while I go fetch your mother?" She smoothed the hair away from his temple where she noticed a scratch that she hadn't seen before.

Marcus nodded. She smiled down at him. "You are so brave, sir. Well done." She patted his shoulder before she hustled from the room. She found Mrs. Bray, Marcus' mother, in short order and they both rushed back to the couch where Marcus lay. The little boy got off quite lucky with only a relatively bad bruise on his leg, nothing broken, and a few various scrapes and bruises.

It wasn't until they were over the first rush of trying to tend to the little boy that Marjorie looked around and realized that Mr. Baeley had disappeared.

"Marcus, where did Mr. Baeley go?" she asked.

He looked up as if nothing were amiss. "He said goodbye and left right after you went to get Mama."

Marjorie frowned as she turned to go to her room. Why had he been here in the first place? How odd. And leaving so unannounced? Strange indeed.

Marjorie was thoroughly nervous. Her stomach quivered with uncertainty and her mind spun with all of the things that could possibly go wrong this evening. Ginger was toying with her hair, sweeping the curls off her face and up into a knot at the back of her head. Daphne was sewing the last few finishing touches to the dress that she had insisted – much to Marjorie's dismay – that Marjorie wear.

"Now, remember that when a conversation lags, you can use one of the subjects we gave you." Ginger encouraged Marjorie around a mouthful of pins that she was jabbing, one by one, into Marjorie's head.

Marjorie nodded, then gasped as a pin went awry and poked into her scalp.

"Don't move!" Ginger squealed, trying to right some of the curls that had fallen.

"Sorry." Marjorie clutched the fan in her lap. She didn't want the girls to know that she had written some of the conversation ideas down on the back of her fan. When it was open, she would be able to read it.

"There!" Daphne stood from her chair in the corner and shook out the dress that had been piled in her lap as she was working on it. It was a lovely golden amber color, very close to the shade of Marjorie's eyes. It shimmered in the light of the lamps that lit the room and Marjorie couldn't help but be a little excited to wear it. It was so pretty. If only it would fit.

"It is lovely, Daphne." Marjorie viewed it as best she could from the mirror as she couldn't turn her head due to Ginger's pinning.

"Ginger! Do hurry up so she can try this on."

"I am hurrying! I'd like to see you do her hair this quickly," Ginger grumbled around her mouthful of pins.

Marjorie stifled a giggle and Daphne tried to look offended, though Marjorie could tell that she was fighting a laugh as well. They all knew that Daphne took forever to do her hair. She had started early this afternoon, shortly after luncheon, in an effort to be ready early so that she could help Marjorie. It had taken her nearly two hours to complete the elaborate style that graced her head with its beauty.

Ginger pushed one more pin into the nest of hair at the back of Marjorie's head and shook out her arms with a heavy sigh. "There!" She took the pins from her mouth and set them in the jar on the vanity table. "Now, let's get you into this dress that Daphne has slaved over for the last two days."

The girls guided Marjorie off the small stool that sat in front of the vanity and held the dress for her. Her corset had already been tightened beyond any hope of breathing normally for the rest of the night. They laced her up the back while having whispered consultations with each other as they fussed with the fabric until it was perfect.

"It fits!" Daphne squealed and clapped her hands. She spun around before coming back to help Ginger finish with the buttons.

"You look beautiful, Marjorie." Ginger spoke from behind her where she was continuing the buttons.

"Really?" Marjorie tried to turn and catch a look of herself in the mirror, but the girls held her in place.

"Ah-ah, no peeking yet!" Daphne flapped her hands at Marjorie and primped the sleeves, helping to get them just a little bit smoother.

Marjorie bounced on her toes, nervous but excited to see what she looked like. She tried not to get her hopes up. She had never looked very pretty. She needed to school her features because if she looked disappointed in any visible way, she would hurt Daphne's feelings. "Thank you so much for working on this dress, Daphne. It was very sweet of you."

"Don't thank me yet, dear. But just you wait until you see yourself," Daphne said with a smug grin.

Marjorie had no idea what she would look like until the girls finally turned her around. She gaped at the girl in the mirror. Somehow the dress suited and flattered her figure far more than anything else she had ever worn. She didn't look plump anymore, just normal. The neck of the gown was cut at a modest, yet flattering, curve that showed off her somehow suddenly graceful neck to full advantage. Silent, she turned slowly this way and that, letting the luminescent silk skirt swish and twinkle in the light.

"Oh, Daphne," she breathed, smoothing the dress with her hands. "How did you?"

Daphne grinned, her beautiful teeth bright in her smiling face. "I told you I was the best seamstress. Though it helped that the dress was already very nice. It is much better made than any of your dresses."

Ginger rolled her eyes at Daphne's bluntness. "Don't mind her," she whispered into Marjorie's ear. But Marjorie was so far over the moon that not one bit of Daphne's bluntness could touch her now.

The distant sound of carriage wheels on gravel sounded through the open windows. Marjorie's heart set to fluttering remarkably fast and she swallowed hard.

Daphne clapped her hands and scurried to check her hair in the mirror. "They're arriving! How do I look?" She primped for a moment then spun, straightening her skirts.

"You look lovely, Daphne, now help me make sure that Marjorie is prepared before we go downstairs. We don't want to make an appearance until at least a few of the carriages arrive anyway."

"Yes, of course. We must make a grand entrance," Daphne agreed, handing Marjorie a pair of white gloves and her fan.

"But, I don't want to make a grand entrance. Couldn't we just blend in?" Marjorie's legs started to quake beneath her beautiful gown.

"Don't be silly, dear." Daphne shook her head.

Lord, help me with this. I am scared. Marjorie threw a prayer heavenward.

They drilled her for a bit longer and her head was so full of rules and ideas that it felt like an overstuffed trunk that couldn't be closed properly.

The time finally arrived for them to go downstairs. As she did her best to glide down the stairs, being extremely careful not to turn her ankle on the heels that she wore, she grew increasingly aware of the number of people below. They milled around and spoke, their voices combining into a soft but overpowering hum. Her legs shook harder, her knees almost knocking together. She hated this. Too many people, too many things to think about. She should have never agreed to this scheme of her companions. Miss Claire met them at the bottom of the stairs and gave them all an approving once-over. She smiled encouragingly at Marjorie and nodded her head.

Marjorie was far too frightened to return the smile. To combat the fear, she quoted the encouragement of her companions in her head. *Mingle with the people, make small talk, engage in conversation.* She could do this.

A gentleman turned towards her with a smile and she felt the blood rush to her head. Never mind. She couldn't do this.

A tug at her elbow alerted her to her friend. Daphne grinned and dragged Marjorie through the crowd towards a small knot of people. "Come on, I'll introduce you."

"W-what about Ginger?" Marjorie stammered. She didn't want to lose sight of her friend on this last day they would get to spend together.

"Oh, I am sure she will be busy trying to say goodbye to everyone." Daphne pulled them to a stop at the small cluster of people she had been headed towards. Marjorie felt herself tremble. These were all young people around Daphne's and her own age. It was much easier to talk with older women; her peers always frightened her.

But there had to be some way to handle this situation appropriately. She took a deep breath.

"You can do this," Daphne whispered before breaking graciously into the conversation.

"Genevieve! How delightful to see you! And, Martha, such a dear." Daphne gushed and embraced each of the girls in turn.

"August Paine." She held out her hand to the young man of the group and fluttered her lashes. Marjorie tried not to roll her eyes.

"A pleasure, madam." August bowed and brushed his lips to her hand.

"Dears, you must meet my dear friend, Marjorie." Daphne gestured to her and she stepped forward. Was it her imagination, or did the other girls' countenance cloud over when they caught sight of Daphne's companion? The older, Genevieve, instantly regained her composure and smiled.

"How do you do, dear?"

Marjorie curtseyed and smiled back. Time for some acting.

"Quite well! A pleasure to make your acquaintance. Lovely weather we have been having, wouldn't you agree?" She tried to smile winningly at Miss Genevieve as she floundered into the conversation head first.

Miss Genevieve looked a little surprised and Martha and August exchanged a glance. A little thrill went through Marjorie. She was doing it!

"Yes, lovely," Genevieve answered and she gestured to her companions. "This is my younger sister, Martha, and my brother, August."

"How do you do?" Marjorie was getting the hang of this. She fluttered her fan, wishing her palms weren't so sweaty beneath her gloves. Why was it so uncommonly hot in here?

They both nodded. "I was trying to discuss the war in America and how it was progressing, but the ladies didn't seem to be interested in such a discussion," August said with a somewhat annoyed tone and expression at his sisters.

"Really? How fascinating!" Marjorie flickered her fan in front of her face. That was probably the first thing she said that hadn't been a bluff. She did find the war fascinating, though she did feel as though her countrymen of England were being a bit pig-headed when it came to politics. Something niggled at the back of her brain when Daphne gave her a frightened stare and the other two women looked somewhat askance. Had she done something wrong? Mercy knows it wouldn't be the least bit surprising if she had.

August's eyes lit up with a small measure of excitement. "Really? I must say I am quite interested to hear your thoughts on the matter, Miss Marjorie. You would be one of the first women I know to take any interest in the matter."

Marjorie caught Daphne shaking her head ever so slightly. What on earth could the girl mean? "Really? How strange. I am sure most women have plenty to say on the subject."

August looked interested. Marjorie was trying to figure out why on earth Daphne was shaking her head so hard.

"And what are your thoughts, Miss Marjorie?" he asked.

"Oh! Excuse me! I see an old friend I simply must talk to." Martha gave Daphne a look, smiled, and bowed out of the group, hurrying away towards another chattering clique of people.

"Well, personally, I think that England is taxing them a bit unfairly." Marjorie fluttered her fan at her face; it was so hot.

Daphne sighed and looked at her feet. Genevieve looked a bit shocked and a fire lit behind August's eyes. "But, you must see, Miss Marjorie, that the colonies must submit to their ruler."

The blood rose in Marjorie's head. "But have they no right to be represented?" Marjorie drew on everything she had read in the papers and learned from Ginger's letters from her father. She thought she certainly knew enough to speak from a place of knowledge. "All of the other towns and major ports have representatives in Parliament, but the American colonies have none. Would you not see that as unfair, Mr. Paine?"

Mr. Paine spluttered slightly and he grew even more strong in his demeanor. He had looked somewhat dismissive when he had asked what her thoughts were on the subject. Perhaps he had thought that she had nothing of importance to say. But now that he saw that he had a fine argument on his hands, he grew hotly argumentative.

Marjorie's blood ran hot. This man was obviously on the side of Parliament, while she was on the side of settling with the Americas peaceably and quickly, deeming them fit to rule their own government, or at least have a say in how it was governed. She supposed it was a matter of pride for a man and it started to get her angry when she argued with him.

August made a particularly strong point for Parliament, "The colonies started this war. Mother England is just trying to finish it!"

Marjorie was startled from replying by a round of applause. She glanced around her and was frightened out of her wits to realize that they had drawn a rather large crowd and now she stood, arguing with a man, and about politics no less. Her cheeks heated and she flipped open her fan out of embarrassment and her eyes snagged on the notes she had written there.

"Don't talk about politics" was written across it plain as day.

She thought she was going to die of either embarrassment, and if not from that, then from blushing.

"Here here!" "Well put!" "Teach those young dogs a lesson!" were some of the things the men around her were saying. Goodness! She had unwittingly started a heated debate and she had made a showpiece out of herself. She looked around her for her companions and saw that Daphne was busy across the room with some of her young friends. Miss Claire and Ginger were nowhere to be seen. What had she gotten herself into?

"Excuse me, gentlemen. But I must say that I agree with Miss Kirk when it comes to the American colonies."

She looked up through her haze of humiliation. There stood Mr. Baeley, the minister, and he was siding with her. She wasn't sure if she should be relieved or even more embarrassed.

But when she looked around, she noticed that most of the people in the room looked suddenly uncomfortable. Through her haze of humiliation, she thought surely no one could be more uncomfortable than she was. Could one die of embarrassment or have their ears burn off from the heat of a blush? She heard people grumbling under their breath. The heat was rushing in her head and her heart was pounding so hard, it felt like a headache. It was only a moment before she realized that some of the crowd had dispersed.

41

By Victoria Lynn

Someone grasped her elbow and pulled her away and out into the open air. The cool air caressed her hot cheeks and she wished that a gale-force wind would blow her over.

"Marjorie, how could you!" Daphne's hiss of a whisper in her ear brought her to her senses and some of the fog cleared.

"I'm so sorry. What happened?" Marjorie grasped her friend's hand, looking imploringly into Daphne's red face and flashing eyes.

"You broke the number one rule." She huffed and pulled her hand away, folding her arms and stepping away to look out over the garden. "I can't believe you brought up politics. Don't you realize? You may very well have ruined the party and after all, we were trying to have a good night for Ginger."

Marjorie tried not to let the tears that had gathered in her eyes fall down her face. "How did I ruin it?"

Daphne turned on her with frustration evident on her face and in her tense voice. "Not only did you bring up politics, which is arguably one of the worst things to discuss at a party, but you brought up one of the most controversial issues of our time! And now, no one knows what to do because the minister disagrees with most of the population, and what could that mean for his career?" Daphne let out a huge huff at the end of her remonstrances.

Marjorie fought back the tears. "I'm sorry." Her voice barely made it out.

"Well, I'd better get back in there and make sure that the whole party hasn't gone to ruin." Daphne turned with a swish of pink silk skirts and disappeared within the bright lights and buzz of conversation, underscored by the ballroom music.

42

Marjorie was left by herself on the portico, her heart breaking and just about as mad at herself as Daphne had been. She was so stupid. She never could do anything right and she now had just mucked up that entire affair. Typical. She never should have thought that she could become a society lady with just a bit of training. It was a lost cause.

But what hurt her even more at this moment was the realization that she had single-handedly ruined Ginger's going away party. Her chest heaving from a combination of her effort to keep from crying and the corset, she moved towards the edge of the portico near the garden and sat down on a bench that graced an area right by the wall. She pulled off her gloves and dug in her reticule for a handkerchief. She had been in such a hurry that she had forgotten to take one from the vanity drawer. Another failure on her part.

"Excuse me, perhaps this would be of service."

She looked up and beheld Mr. Baeley, the minister, holding out his handkerchief to her. Here she sat, a blubbering mess. She was doomed to remain in absolute misery every time they met. She might as well accept it at this point.

She took the handkerchief, trying to keep herself from blushing. It was one thing to tell herself that she should no longer feel embarrassed, and another to actually do it.

He stood silently by as she dabbed at her eyes and tried to get herself under control. The thought of Ginger leaving was enough to make the tears start brimming again. She hated herself for being so uncontrollable in front of the minister. "Please . . . excuse me," she choked out as she stood hastily, and with barely a bob for a curtsey, she rushed into the house and up the stairs to her bedroom.

There was no use in heading back to the party. She had made a nuisance of herself and she couldn't keep herself from crying long enough to be in the least bit sociable. No sooner did she dry her tears and pat some powder on her face before they again filled her eyes and spilled down her cheeks. She gave up and undressed out of the gorgeous gown that Daphne had provided for her. Crawling into bed, she realized how terribly she had behaved. She had brought up one of the worst issues to discuss in polite conversation. She chided herself over and over. How could she have been so stupid?

"Lord, I feel silly asking for help. Who needs to ask God for help with social interactions? I feel so ridiculous. Like I don't belong. I don't know what to do, I just wish –" she floundered in her words. While praying, she always felt it so easy to converse from her heart. Something she never felt with anyone besides occasionally Miss Claire. It took her quite a while to open up to others, and it must be someone she trusted. Thankfully, the Lord seldom seemed to share any of her secrets with others. He was the perfect confidant. Always ready and available, always comforting, and always respectful.

Tears started to her eyes. "Lord, I just want to feel like everyone else. I am tired of being by myself. I feel lonely. No one seems to care that I exist. Everyone loves Daphne and Ginger, but I am the odd duck." She pulled a handkerchief from under her pillows and mopped her eyes. The Lord breathed a bit of peace into her heart, and it wasn't long before she drifted off to sleep.

Saying goodbye to Ginger was terribly difficult. The girls had been together for several years and Ginger had naturally grown closer to Marjorie than Daphne had. They had similar temperaments and enjoyed each other's company. But, now they would have to rely solely on letters in order to communicate. Marjorie had hidden herself away in the garden for a good cry with the now half-bloomed roses. Their soft, adolescent faces helped to cheer her breaking heart. She was happy for Ginger, she really was, but she hated when others had to move on. It made it even more difficult when she was left behind. It was just another reminder of how she was different.

She noticed a weed in the garden bed below her feet and she stooped to pluck it from its home. Pulling herself together, she sniffed and dabbed her handkerchief at her nose. These roses really needed to be trimmed. With determination in her step and the hope that she would chase away her gloomy thoughts by working, she headed towards the workshed. A little voice startled her.

"Miss Marjorie! What are you doing?" Little Marcus ran up to her, a paper cap on his head, a wooden sword in hand, and a quizzical, excited look on his face.

She hoped that he wouldn't notice that she had been crying. She smiled when the sight of his sword filled her mind with an idea. "Marcus, I am on a crusade."

His eyes lit up. "Really?" He trotted along to keep up.

"Yes, you see, the rose garden has been attacked by an enemy that has attached itself to the rose towns. So each bush, I mean town, has some branches that need to be cut away and dragged to the burn pile." She paused in her steps and bent down closer to his ear, looking around as if afraid of being heard. "They are like pirates. They take all of the energy from the whole bush and if we don't trim them away, the bush will wilt."

Marcus nodded solemnly. "Can I help?"

She nodded just as solemnly and took his hand. "Hurry, we must fortify ourselves with weapons."

She spent several hours working with Marcus on the garden, cutting away and pruning the bad branches of the rose bushes. She couldn't wait for them to finish blooming. This section of the garden would be quite the sight to see. They both wandered into the house, dirty, dusty, hot and happy. They entered through the parlor side door and Marjorie stopped mid-giggle when she caught sight of Miss Claire and Mr. Baeley, who rose from his spot on the sofa where he had been sharing tea with Miss Claire.

"Miss Kirk." He bowed.

She felt a blush heat her face. This was becoming a habit of appearing awkward in his presence. "Mr. Baeley. If you will excuse us, we both need to wash up. I am sorry for intruding, I didn't realize we had company." Marjorie started to lead Marcus from the room. Her steps were arrested by a soft touch on her arm.

"Wait, excuse me, Miss Kirk. I have something of yours." He withdrew her fan from the other night from the pocket of his jacket. "You left it on the bench on the portico when you left the other night."

Oh no! All of her society notes were on the back of that fan. What must he think of her?

"Thank you." She reached for it and took it in her dirt-encrusted fingers. She glanced up at him and caught a look of understanding in his eyes. Not quite sure what to do with it, she turned suddenly and made for the door, dragging poor Marcus in her wake.

"Come back when you are cleaned up, Marjorie," Miss Claire called after her before Marjorie closed the door. Marjorie sighed . . . now she would have to help entertain Mr. Baeley. And after her humiliation last night and with Ginger gone, she was not feeling her best. Where in all of England was Daphne? That girl was never where she was needed.

"Miss Marjorie!" puffed little Marcus at her side.

She paused and looked down at him. "Yes, Marcus?" she asked with a distracted glance his direction.

"Could you slow down?"

She shook her head to clear the cobwebs. "I am sorry, Marcus, why don't you run to the kitchen and find your mother? It was such fun working in the garden with you. Those rose pirates won't be back for a long time I think." She smiled and gave him a wink before she turned to the stairs, but not before catching his infectious grin.

In her room, she poured some water in the basin and splashed the dirt away. She grimaced at her fingernails and the dirt that was underneath them. She had forgotten to wear gloves again. Once she had made herself presentable, she checked the girls' rooms for Daphne. No such luck. She grimaced. That left her alone to do the honors of entertaining Mr. Baeley. Of course Miss Claire would be there, but Daphne was always good for conversation. She glanced out one of the magnificent windows of the lovely old house and caught sight of one of Daphne's dresses. She pulled herself to a stop and leaned out the open window, squinting to get a better view.

Daphne was sitting on a bench far out in the garden with a man, talking intently. Marjorie frowned. Did she have a chaperone? And who on earth was she talking to? She sighed. She would need to tell Miss Claire, who would probably leave Marjorie to entertain Mr. Baeley for a moment by herself.

Sure enough, Miss Claire excused herself for a moment and Marjorie stared at her folded hands in her lap. She twisted her fingers around her thumb and worked them hard. Should she say something about last night? She had left him so abruptly.

"Miss Kirk?"

Marjorie looked up for a brief second of recognition, then looked back at her hands.

"Miss Claire left so that I could have the benefit of asking you a question in private."

Confused, Marjorie's gaze flashed to his face. He looked somewhat nervous, but still in control of the situation. He was so strong. So confident. The opposite of what she was.

He cleared his throat. "You see, I asked Miss Claire if I might get to know you better. Ahem." He pulled at his collar. "And, perhaps, would you be willing to enter a courtship with me?"

She stared at him for a moment, taking a bit to realize what he had just asked. Her? Marjorie Kirk? With no wealth, no social standing, and even less social graces? The wife of a minister? *Well, not a wife yet, calm yourself.*

"But . . . Why would you want me? No one wants me. No one cares, I –" She stumbled over her words. "I'm too silly. I can't –" She hid her face in her hands. It was hard to bear the curse of her all-but-smooth tongue.

"I am sure you are quite wrong when you say no one wants you. Don't you know how lovingly Miss Claire speaks of you? And of course little Marcus loves you dearly, have you seen the way he looks at you?"

She felt the tears start to her eyes. "But, last night . . ."

"What about last night?"

"I can't do – the – being social isn't something I can claim to be adept at." There, that sounded somewhat intelligent.

"And how does that make you inferior?"

She spluttered. "I – but, what do you –?"

"You have many other desirable qualities, more so than those who are 'adept at the social graces' as you put it. You are kind, you seem to love children, and despite your claims, you have a very intelligent mind."

She blinked, wide-eyed at him. "How on earth could you have gleaned that in just a few short weeks?" She stared at him aghast.

He smiled, a lovely, gentle smile. "I can be very observant, Miss Kirk."

She recalled all of the times that he had come to dinner, the times when he had caught her in the garden, or helping in the kitchen. Or when he had found her once in the garden, comforting Daphne over some crushed hope. He had noticed

49

her despite the fact that when they were together, she was quiet, awkward, and a wallflower.

"You don't have to change yourself, Miss Kirk. God made you to be the way you are, you needn't try to be anything different than that."

Marjorie looked down at her hands again. Perhaps she had been looking at this all wrong in the first place. Instead of berating herself and looking upon her shortcomings as total failures, she had failed to see that perhaps God had made her this way in the first place. She had been focusing on the things that she was terrible at and despairing over them, instead of seeing the things that she was good at. Mr. Baeley obviously saw something attractive in her personality. Perhaps being beautiful wasn't about being lovely to look at and a good conversationalist. Perhaps it was something a bit more than that. Something broader. What if being beautiful was about being someone who stayed true to the way God made them?

She looked up at the reverend, her eyes starting to smart with tears. She never thought anyone would ever look at her in that way. Is this how God saw her? As something precious, to be desired and beautiful? "Courtship . . . ," she breathed.

"Indeed, Miss Kirk."

Seven years later . . .

Marjorie comforted her little daughter and kissed the knee that had been scraped while on some wild escapade out of doors. She stood and set the consoled child back on her feet.

The child then ran from the room as if nothing had happened to mar her day in the least. Marjorie patted her swollen abdomen and moved towards the kitchen. This new life nestled beneath her heart would be her fourth little one in the six years she had been married to the Reverend William Baeley.

She smiled to herself as she gathered her gardening gloves, jammed her straw hat on her head and headed out to the garden. She gasped with delight when she caught sight of the rose arbor. Just last night they had been buds of many different sizes, and this morning the entire arbor was in full bloom, the roses sending out their gorgeous fragrance and the full red and pink blossoms were stunning in their profuseness. She placed a hand over her heart. Such beauty.

A hand touched the small of her back and a kiss was planted gently on her cheek. "Good morning, my lovely wife." She turned to catch her husband's look of love and admiration. She smoothed down the skirts of her blush linen gown. He caught her hands and turned her towards him.

"Good morning. Aren't they beautiful?" She cast her eyes in the direction of the roses, breathless with their beauty.

"They are indeed, though not nearly as beautiful as my wife in full bloom."

She smiled and let him pull her to his side as they surveyed the garden and the early morning sun that cast its bright rays over the garden. Five-year-old Ginger chased little William through the beds of perennials, their giggles like music to their parents' ears.

They had worked hard to make this piece of earth a paradise. The little parsonage had become as homey as

Marjorie could make it and the garden was as welcoming as the house, if not more so. While being the wife of the reverend did entail some socializing, Marjorie had learned to delegate as much as possible and to be calm when delegating it was no longer an option. There were generally plenty of the parish ladies who loved leading and heading up social events, but Marjorie had also learned to be a little more comfortable in such situations. She was still learning to accept the fact that she wasn't perfect and to relax when she was failing instead of berating herself.

She found her fulfillment in living the way God had made her. She was good at being a mother, teaching the children's Sunday school, conversing one-on-one with the other women and encouraging them. She loved to do handiwork and many a woman in the village had a little blanket made by the hands of the reverend's wife.

Much like these flowers, she had come to a place of bloom. She felt at peace with her life and the way she lived it. Her heart sang when she was doing the things that she was gifted in. Looking at the roses now, something her husband had told her a few years after their marriage came to her mind.

Beauty blooms when you are true to who God created you to be.

The End

When Beauty Blooms

A Letter from the Author

Dear reader,

Thank you so much for reading my book! I am so blessed that you chose to read it!

I love hearing from my readers, so if you have any questions or just want to chat, you can contact me at: www.victorialynnauthor.com/contact

Also, reviews really help me, even if they are short. If you could leave a brief review on my amazon page, that would be amazing and you would have my undying gratitude!

May the Lord bless you and keep you!

By God's Grace,

Victoria Lynn

Acknowledgements

I would first and foremost like to thank my Lord and Savior for giving me the gifting and the passion as well as the stories.

Many thanks to my blog readers who read a writing prompt and begged for more. Your excitement and encouragement was one of the main reasons I chose to continue on with Marjorie's saga.

Thank you to my family for their encouragement and support. You all mean more to me than anything. Thank you Sarah Grace and Isabella for being the best cheerleaders and for always being so excited to read my stories.

Thank you to all of my Beta readers for the advice and new perspectives on this story. Jesseca Wheaton, Grace Gidman, Sarah Grace, and Rebecca G. You all were invaluable.

Thank you to Bridget Marshall who not only proofread this story but also gave me encouragement and invaluable help with all of the nitty gritty of punctuation that I am too flighty to take on.

Thank you so much to my Alpha readers, Beth and Angela who gave me such encouraging initial feedback that I couldn't wait to polish her up and get her ready for the world.

And thank you to all of those who will read this book. You are beautiful just the way God created you to be!

To God alone be the glory,

Victoria Lynn

Also by Victoria Lynn:

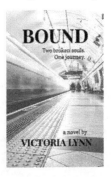

Two souls don't find each other by simple accident.
~ Jorge Luis Borges ~

Levi thought he was making this journey alone. But when he meets a ten-year-old girl at the train station, that plan is turned on its head.

Casey is running away and finds out that Levi is, too. They decide to journey together and their lives are suddenly bound together in a journey they will not soon forget.

Both children come from abusive situations and are running from the dangers of their previous life. Levi is confident he can handle this on his own, but when Casey is injured on the journey, he must seek help from the first person that comes into his path—or rather, people. Mr. and Mrs. Bellworth are simple farm folk with a heart for kids and a passion for serving God. When their unconditional love and gentle care surrounds Levi and Casey, the troubles of their previous lives melt away and they start to flourish. But when Casey is dragged back into the abusive world she came from, the emotional trauma, pain, and distrust resurfaces. Will they be forever bound by their past? Or will God answer their prayers?

Available in paperback and eBook on Amazon . . .

London In The Dark

London, 1910

Budding Private Detective Cyril Arlington Hartwell has a conundrum. London is being ravaged by the largest run of thefts in recent history. His hunch that it is all tied together may put him and those he loves in more danger than he could have reckoned.

Olivia Larken Hartwell is just home from boarding school for the summer anticipating time with her adoring parents. She misses her absent brother, Cyril, hoping for the day he will finally come home. But tragedy strikes, causing upheaval for all concerned and changes her life in a way she never could have imagined.

Olivia, Cyril, and their friends must bring the hidden to light, seek to execute justice, and dispel the darkness that hovers over London... and their hearts.

Available on Amazon

in paperback and e-book form.

VICTORIA LYNN is in her 20s and if she's not writing, she is probably sewing, singing, playing the piano, washing dishes, creating something with her hands, or learning something new. She has a passion for serving her Creator, encouraging others, and being creative. She blogs at www.rufflesandgrace.com about writing, fashion, modesty, her walk with God, and life. She lives in Michigan with her parents and 8 siblings.

Made in the USA
Columbia, SC
20 July 2024